HAPPY HIDING HIPPOS

by Bobette McCarthy

Bradbury Press • **New York**

Maxwell Macmillan Canada • *Toronto*
Maxwell Macmillan International
New York • *Oxford* • *Singapore* • *Sydney*

Bradbury Press
Macmillan Publishing Company
866 Third Avenue
New York, NY 10022

Maxwell Macmillan Canada, Inc.
1200 Eglinton Avenue East
Suite 200
Don Mills, Ontario M3C 3N1

Macmillan Publishing Company is part of the Maxwell Communication
Group of Companies.

First edition
Printed and bound in Singapore
10 9 8 7 6 5 4 3 2 1
The text of this book is set in 24-point Cheltenham Book.
The illustrations are rendered in watercolor.

LIBRARY OF CONGRESS CATALOGING-IN-PUBLICATION DATA
McCarthy, Bobette.
Happy hiding hippos / by Bobette McCarthy.—1st ed.
p.   cm.
Summary: Jolly hippos play a rambunctious game of hide-and-seek
all over town.
ISBN 0-02-765446-X
[1. Hippopotamus—Fiction. 2. Hide-and-seek—Fiction. 3. Stories
in rhyme.] I. Title.
PZ8.3.M4593Hap 1994
[E]—dc20   92-32599

To Hallie and Matthew,
with love

Happy hiding hippos are hiding everywhere.

In the kitchen, in the tub,
they're hiding here and there.

In the cellar, on the stairs,
and way up in the attic—

sometimes hiding hippos
are downright acrobatic.

This one thinks he is a lamp,
although he needs some practice.

This one is a bouncing ball; this one is a cactus.

On the porch, into the yard, racing out the door,

happy hiding hippos will stay at home no more.

Slower-moving hippos and running ones collide.

Everyone should step aside
when happy hippos hide!

Down the streets and through the shops,
in and out they zoom.

When happy hippos hide,
we all must make some room.

Tiny hippos, tall ones too,
have smiles both big and wide,

and cranky hippos are no match
when happy hippos hide.

For hiding spots, what better place
than a peaceful park?

Hippos plan to play and hide
until the park is dark.... *But*

Hippos of all kinds agree
that one thing is quite plain:

the park is just no place to hide
when it begins to rain.

They're getting tired, slowing down,
this one has bumped her head.

Perhaps it's time
that hiding hippos
headed off to bed.

When hiding hippos settle down,
you cannot hear a peep.

The world is such a quiet place
when happy hippos sleep.